NIGHT OF THE WEREWOLF

**Don't miss these upcoming
CHOOSE YOUR OWN**

titles from Bantam Books:

**#2
Beware the Snake's Venom**

**#3
Island of Doom**

CHOOSE YOUR OWN

NIGHTMARE... #1

NIGHT OF THE WEREWOLF
BY EDWARD PACKARD

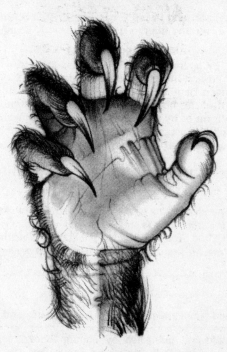

ILLUSTRATED BY BILL SCHMIDT

A BANTAM BOOK
NEW YORK·TORONTO·LONDON·SYDNEY·AUCKLAND

RL 4, age 008-012

NIGHT OF THE WEREWOLF
A Bantam Book/April 1995

CHOOSE YOUR OWN NIGHTMARE is a series by
Bantam Doubleday Dell Books
for Young Readers,
a division of Bantam Doubleday Dell Publishing Group, Inc.

Cover art and inside illustrations by Bill Schmidt
Cover and interior design by Beverly Leung

ISBN 0-553-48229-7

Published simultaneously in the United States and Canada

Bantam Books are published by Bantam Books, a division of
Bantam Doubleday Dell Publishing Group, Inc. Its trademark,
consisting of the words "Bantam Books" and the portrayal of a
rooster, is Registered in U.S. Patent and Trademark Office and in
other countries. Marca Registrada. Bantam Books, 1540 Broadway,
New York, New York 10036.

PRINTED IN THE UNITED STATES OF AMERICA

OPM   0   9   8   7   6   5   4   3   2   1

NIGHT OF THE WEREWOLF

WARNING!

You have probably read books where scary things happen to people. Well, in *Choose Your Own Nightmare,* you're right in the middle of the action. The scary things are happening to you!

So get ready for a vacation you won't forget—dead bodies, dark nights—and a howling, prowling werewolf!

Fortunately, while you're reading along you'll have chances to decide what to do. Whenever you make a decision, turn to the page shown. The thrills and chills that happen to you next will depend on your choices.

Make sure to choose carefully. Or who knows? You may have a werewolf to keep you company!

It's summer vacation, and you're on your way to visit your cousins, Karin and Tom, in their new house. Your aunt Charlotte is waiting for you at the bus depot. She gives you a big smile and a hug, but she doesn't look happy. You wonder if something's wrong.

Later, driving home, she catches your eye. "There's something you should know," she says. "The police found a body yesterday—it was by a pond only half a mile from our house."

"Wow, that's terrible! Was it a murder?" you ask.

"They don't know. The victim was covered with deep bites, as if he'd been attacked by a dog with huge teeth. But there aren't any dogs like that around here."

"That's weird," you say, shaking your head.

Aunt Charlotte slows down and then turns onto a narrow, winding road. "Yes, it *is* weird," she says. "And I've told Karin and Tom —and I'm telling you—be very careful where you go. Stay together and keep your eyes open for trouble."

Turn to page 2.

"You don't need to tell me," you say, though you're feeling more curious than scared.

A few moments later your aunt swings the car into the driveway and pulls up in front of a white frame house half hidden by pine trees. Aunt Charlotte looks over at you. "This is what we call home. What do you think of it?"

"Nice," you say. The house looks as if it needs a coat of paint, but it has a screened porch with rocking chairs and a hammock. There's a small upstairs porch, too. A crow is sitting on the railing. It caws loudly as if to make sure you notice it.

Your aunt starts into the house. You grab your duffel bag and follow her inside. Karin races downstairs, with Tom right behind her.

"Hi!" Karin says, giving you a hug.

The phone is ringing, so Aunt Charlotte goes to answer it. Your cousins show you to the guest room. You throw your duffel bag on the bed and wash up. A few moments later you join your cousins in the den.

Go on to the next page.

"Did Mom tell you?" Tom asks when you come in.

"About the murder?"

"Yeah, but also about the suspect?" Karin says.

"No. Do they know who did it?"

Tom and Karin exchange glances. "Not exactly," Karin says. "They think it was some weirdo who used to live around here."

"But your mom said there were big teeth marks."

"That's what's *really* weird," Karin exclaims. "It's as if the murderer was a werewolf or something."

Turn to page 4.

4

"We'd better investigate this," Tom says. As he's speaking, you notice a fat book in the bookshelf. It's titled *Encyclopedia of the Supernatural*. The book is very old—you're almost afraid it will crumble in your hands. Carefully, you pull it down from the shelf.

You thumb through the book until you reach the letter "W." "Here—'werewolf,' " you announce.

Tom and Karin crowd around you. "What does it say?" Tom asks.

You read out loud:

Werewolf: A person who is changed into a wolf, and who begins to look and act like one. No one knows why this happens. But we do know that a werewolf is very strong and very dangerous, especially when it is hungry. Some experts say that a witch can destroy a werewolf. It might even be possible for an ordinary person to overcome one, but it would be very unwise to try. The safest way to deal with a werewolf is to get as far away from it as possible.

"This gives me the shivers," Karin says.

Go on to the next page.

"That's all the more reason to check things out," Tom says. "I'm going over to Paulding's Pond—that's where they found the body."

"The police have already been there," Karin says.

"It won't hurt to go again," her brother replies. "We might find something they missed."

"Well, I'm not going anywhere near that pond," Karin says. "I've got a better idea. I'm going to go talk to Mrs. Hadley down the road. Maybe she's seen something like this before."

"That old crazy!" Tom scoffs.

"That old crazy is just the sort of person who would know about werewolves," Karin says calmly.

Tom looks at you. "Well, I'm going to check out the pond. Want to come?"

"Or you can come with me and talk to Mrs. Hadley," Karin offers.

If you decide to visit Mrs. Hadley with Karin, turn to page 20.

If you decide to investigate the pond with Tom, turn to page 34.

6

"Mom, he was in the house!" Karin cries. "Trying to get in my room! We had to jump out the window!" She's leaning forward against the back of Tom's seat. Aunt Charlotte half-turns and gives her a quick hug. "It's okay now, honey." She slams the car into reverse, backs out of the driveway, and races down the road.

"Where are we going, Mom?" asks Tom.

"To the police station—where else?" says Aunt Charlotte, and turns a corner so fast that only your seat belt keeps you from being thrown against the door.

An hour later you are back at Aunt Charlotte's house, this time with a policeman. The storm has passed. The state police have been called in, and troopers are combing the area, looking for the strange intruder.

With Aunt Charlotte and your cousins, you lead the policeman up and show him Karin's room. The door that the werewolf forced open is scuffed and dented. Karin's bed frame is split down its entire length.

The policeman shakes his head. "We'll get him, ma'am. You can be sure of that."

Turn to page 21.

Keeping low, you slip into the water, wishing it weren't so cold. When it's deep enough, you dive and start swimming for the opposite shore. It's summertime, and you're only wearing shorts, a T-shirt, and beat-up sneakers. Still, they're heavy once they're wet. About halfway across, you have to slow down to catch your breath.

At that moment you feel a sharp pain in your leg. A snapping turtle is trying to take a piece of you! You bat the turtle off with your hand and swim hard for the nearest shore. Even the pain in your leg and the weight of your wet clothing can't stop you from making record time.

When you reach the pond's edge, you find that you're right at the roped-off crime scene. And a policeman is waiting for you! A German shepherd sits obediently at his side.

You climb up the grassy bank. The policeman starts giving you a lecture about trespassing, but when he sees you're bleeding, he breaks off.

"We'd better get something on that leg," he says. "C'mon."

Turn to page 51.

8

"Who is that?" a voice screams. It's coming from one of the windows.

"It's Charlotte from down the road," your aunt calls out. "We wanted to make sure you were all right."

"Well, you shouldn't be snooping around," Mrs. Hadley replies.

"I'm sorry," Aunt Charlotte says, a little annoyed. "I didn't mean—"

Mrs. Hadley cuts her off. "What were you worried about? Come around to the kitchen door, if you're so curious." A few seconds later she lets all of you in.

"Now, what's this about making sure I'm all right?" she demands. She is holding a teacup, which she waves angrily as she talks.

None of you can answer. You're staring at a creature stretched out on the floor. It has a shaggy coat of hair. Its hands and feet are padded paws. Its face is long and pointed, and its nose is round, black, and moist. The creature's long mouth is half open, revealing long, sharp-pointed teeth. *It's the werewolf!*

Turn to page 19.

10

At dinnertime, Karin tells about the weird conversation she had with Mrs. Hadley. You and Tom tell about your adventures at Paulding's Pond. Then everyone makes up funny stories about werewolves, but the fact is that you are all a little nervous—even Aunt Charlotte. After all, the murderer, whether a werewolf or not, still hasn't been caught.

"I think we should do something to get our minds off this," Aunt Charlotte says.

"Let's get a movie," Karin says.

Everyone likes this idea. Without even finishing the dishes, you all pile into the car, and Aunt Charlotte drives you to Movieworld. Once there, you start looking over the titles.

Tom picks one up and waves it triumphantly. It's called *Night of the Werewolf*.

Aunt Charlotte, eyeing it, says, "I thought we were going to get our minds off that."

But you, Tom, and Karin all say you want it, so Aunt Charlotte rents it. When you get home, she pops some popcorn. As soon as it's ready, you all get comfortable on the sofa. Tom turns down the lights, and Karin starts the movie.

Turn to page 22.

You and Karin start down the road from Mrs. Hadley's house. Lightning flashes. A moment later thunder rumbles across the sky. It's going to rain any minute, but you're not thinking about that. You're thinking about Mrs. Hadley. Something about her really gives you the creeps.

Between that and thinking about the werewolf, you feel like running all the way home. But you don't want to let yourself act so frightened, so you just walk fast. Judging by how Karin keeps up with you, you guess she feels the same way you do.

You pass the dirt road leading through the woods to Paulding's Pond. It's almost dark, and you can only see a little way in before the road disappears into the shadows. Suddenly a flash of lightning reveals two figures on the road. One of them is large, stooped, and shaggy looking. The other is a boy.

Turn to page 41.

12

He scowls at you and curls his tongue over his enormous teeth. "If you ever want to leave, you will try my soup!" Hearing him say this makes you want to throw it in his face!

"NOW!" he screams.

You shrink back, thinking he'll force the soup on you, but instead he reaches over and rips a leg off the remains of the rabbit. He gnaws at it, eyeing you while he eats.

Then he throws what's left of the rabbit bone into the pot and stares at you, making the soft, purring sound again. He shoves the bowl almost under your nose. "You must try this!" he says. "You will *try* it!"

The idea of having any of his soup is revolting. But you have a feeling that if you don't get out of this place soon, it may be *your* bones that end up in the next bowl!

Maybe you'll just have to take a taste— either that or do something desperate. Maybe you *should* throw the soup at him and make a run for it.

If you try the soup, turn to page 39.

If you throw the soup at the werewolf and make a run for it, turn to page 54.

"No, we've got to escape!" you say. You open the window and climb up on the sill. You beckon to Karin. "C'mon, the tree is right here!"

AWAAARRREEEEEEEEEeeeeee!

The werewolf is in the bedroom! He moves so fast that you can't get a good look. But there's no way you can miss his snarls and growls.

"Karin!" you scream, reaching for your terrified cousin. "Follow me!" You jump, but you weren't quite ready. You can't get a grip on the tree. *You're falling!*

Turn to page 85.

14

"Nothing," Karin says. "But the police found a body by Paulding's Pond. There were huge teeth marks on it—like wolf bites—and deep scratches."

Mrs. Hadley's jaw drops, her eyes widen, and she pulls back a step. "A murder? *Really!*" Her eyes seem to be searching beyond you for a moment. "I think you'd better come in, children. There is something you should know."

You and Karin follow Mrs. Hadley through her strange little living room. Wooden trunks are stacked along the walls. There's a grandfather clock with no hands and a tiny fireplace that has been sealed with cement. A door at the back of the living room leads directly to the kitchen. The two rooms seem to take up the whole house. You wonder where Mrs. Hadley sleeps.

The old woman tells you to sit at the table and brings over a pot of tea from the counter. After pouring the tea, she sits down across from you, eyeing you over the rim of her cup as she drinks. The tea has an odd smell to it, like water in the bottom of a vase of dead flowers.

Turn to page 23.

Even as she speaks, you hear a *pat, pat, pat* on the stairs. It's not the sound of shoes. It's the sound of padded feet!

"We've got to barricade the door," Karin says. "Help me move my bed in front of it!"

AWAAARRREEEEEEEEEEeeeeeeee! From the top of the stairs!

"The bed may not stop it!" you scream. "We can shinny down the tree outside the window."

"It's too far to jump. Help me!" Karin starts tugging at the bed frame, but she's not strong enough to move it by herself.

*If you help Karin barricade the door,
turn to page 32.*

*If you insist on leaping to the tree,
turn to page 13.*

You and Tom step inside. There's a sink, a woodstove, a bed, a table, and a couple of straight-back chairs that remind you of the ones in Aunt Charlotte's house. The floor under the sink is littered with bones, small ones that look like chicken or maybe rabbit bones, and some larger ones. You stare at them.

Tom gasps. "Are those deer bones or . . . ?"

"Or human." You bend down to look more closely.

Tom is peering through the window. *"He's coming!"*

Turn to page 33.

"Oh, he had a mouth, all right," Mrs. Hadley says, her voice rising. "And jaws. That's what I remember most. I was in my garden, and I saw him staring at me through the woods. He looked at me as if I were a slab of steak on his plate. I didn't like it. And I thought, 'Someday he'll learn not to look at me like that!'" She leans closer. "You see, children, I was already beginning to learn about my special powers!"

Hearing this strange talk, you remember how Tom had said Mrs. Hadley was crazy.

"Who owned our house then?" Karin asks.

"A Mr. Roger Cranmore." As she says this, a Siamese cat leaps up on the table. It looks at you with cold, blue-gray eyes.

"Did you know Mr. Cranmore?" you ask.

"Very slightly—he traveled a great deal," says Mrs. Hadley, stroking her cat. "He was murdered right in his own bed." Karin's eyes widen. "His body was found by the police after he didn't show up at work," Mrs. Hadley continues.

Turn to page 31.

How did this happen? you wonder. It's the strangest sight you ever saw! But, even stranger, the werewolf is dissolving in front of your eyes! Its snout is shriveling. Its shaggy coat is shrinking, as if the flesh and bones underneath were disappearing into thin air. Then the creature's skin vanishes, leaving a thick pattern of coarse, bristly hairs on the floor, forming the outline of the body that is no longer there.

This can't be happening! You must be dreaming! But then you remember reading in the encyclopedia about what can destroy a werewolf, and you look over at Mrs. Hadley. She has a wild look in her eyes. She rubs her hands. Her cat suddenly jumps on her shoulder. It stares at you coldly.

Turn to page 30.

"I want to hear what Mrs. Hadley has to say," you tell Tom. "Come on, Karin, let's go."

A few minutes later you and Karin knock on the door of Mrs. Hadley's house, a tiny cottage perched on a grassy knoll at the edge of the woods. You wait for a minute or so, but there's no answer.

You glance around. The sun is dipping beneath the trees. Long shadows reach out from the woods and cover the ground.

"She's always home," Karin says. "I think she's kind of deaf." She starts banging harder. You knock a couple of times yourself.

A face appears at the window. A moment later an old woman with long white hair, a thin face, and piercing blue eyes opens the door. She glares at you and speaks in a harsh, crackly voice. "What do you want, children? Making such a racket!"

"We were wondering if you'd seen anything strange around here lately, a weird man, or a creature?" Karin asks.

Mrs. Hadley jerks back, her already wrinkled brow wrinkling even more. "What have you seen?" she demands.

Turn to page 14.

"I'm not sure it's a 'him,' " Aunt Charlotte says. "From what the kids say, it may be an 'it.' "

The policeman squints at her a moment. "Well, whether it's a 'him' or an 'it,' the chief thinks he might come back. He wants me to spend the night here and keep an eye on things. Meanwhile, don't anyone go in this room. The detective will be here in the morning to go over it for fingerprints."

And clawprints, you think.

"You can sleep on the daybed in the spare room," Aunt Charlotte says to Karin. She puts her arm around her. "We'll get your room fixed up, honey," she says.

The policeman sits in the kitchen drinking coffee. The rest of you gather in the living room and talk about what happened.

Aunt Charlotte picks up the phone and dials a number. After a few moments she hangs up, looking concerned. "I thought I'd call Mrs. Hadley and tell her to lock her place up extra tight, but there's no answer."

Turn to page 50.

22

The film begins with the camera panning over a forest. A long, wailing howl fills the air. Somewhere in those woods there's a were-wolf!

The camera zooms in on a family inside a house. The parents and their kids are sitting around the TV. The same howl you heard a moment ago fills the room. A little girl runs to the window.

"What's that?" her brother asks.

"I don't know," says the father.

The girl starts back, but then you hear the howling again, much closer. There's a pounding on the door and the lights in the family's room start flickering.

"Who's that at the door?" the boy asks. No one answers him.

The pounding and growling continue.

The father gets up.

The mother pulls at his sleeve. "John, don't go to the door. Call the police!"

The father grabs the phone and dials a number. The pounding continues. There's the sound of splitting wood—the door is being broken down!

Turn to page 63.

"Now where shall I begin?" Mrs. Hadley says. "I never expected to talk about this, but I think that it's time." She narrows her eyes and purses her lips, staring at you so hard you shrink back in your chair.

"Years ago," she says, "there was a man who lived in the woods behind your house, Karin. There was a shack back there. Everyone assumed he lived in it, but almost no one ever saw him."

"Did you ever see him?" you ask.

She nods, pouring more of the smelly tea into her cup. "Only once. He had a short, ragged beard, bristly hair, and a pointed face with a long, thick nose that seemed to join with his chin."

"How was there room for his mouth?" asks Karin.

Turn to page 18.

You scramble into the thick brush, trying to make as little noise as possible. You strain your ears, listening. It's really quiet. Then you hear the sound of footsteps again. Whatever it is, it's moving off to the left.

Maybe it's going away, you think. But a second later you hear it again, this time moving toward you. It's big—you can tell that. And it doesn't sound human.

You hear it coming closer . . . closer . . . Your heart races. It's almost on you now—it must know right where you are! You cringe, covering your head with your arms.

Suddenly it's upon you! You smell its hot, foul breath. Its huge paw is on your arm. You are shielding your face, but through your fingers you get a glimpse of its jaws about to close on your neck.

"STAY!" A voice calls. *"BACK!"*

The creature backs away from you. Still cringing, you look up into the soft brown eyes of a German shepherd. Behind the dog stands a stern-faced policeman.

You're still alive, but you have a feeling your troubles have just begun.

The End

26

Karin reaches her mother on the phone, and a few minutes later she comes to get you. On the way home, you tell her what Mrs. Hadley said. She laughs.

"A werewolf? Ridiculous. Ellen Hadley is getting crazier every year. Making up a story like that—trying to scare you. She should be ashamed of herself. Except I'm sure she can't help it. She's always been a strange woman, and I guess the older she gets the stranger she gets." Aunt Charlotte turns into the driveway and pulls to a stop. You and Karin follow her inside the house.

"Tom," she calls. There's no answer.

"He went down to Paulding's Pond, where they found the body," Karin says. "Guess he's not back yet."

A startled look comes over your aunt's face, as if she believes in werewolves after all. "Well it's getting quite dark—it could rain any minute," she says.

Turn to page 79.

"I don't want to miss anything. I'll come along," you say.

You, Tom, and Karin all pile into the car. A few minutes later Aunt Charlotte pulls up in front of Mrs. Hadley's cottage. There's only a single dim light on, coming from her kitchen.

"You kids better stay in the car—and lock it," Aunt Charlotte says.

"No way," Tom replies. He opens the door and hops out. Just as fast, you and Karin are out the other side.

"All right," Aunt Charlotte says. "Just stay together, and stay close to me."

You all follow her up to the front door. She bangs loudly. There's no answer.

"She's kind of deaf," Tom says.

"Maybe she's afraid to open it," you say.

"Mrs. Hadley!" Aunt Charlotte yells, rapping again.

"Let's look in the kitchen window. That's the only room with a light on," you say.

"Follow me," Aunt Charlotte says. The four of you start around the corner of the house.

Turn to page 8.

Looking into the kitchen, you see the policeman sitting at the table reading a magazine and drinking coffee. Not a great way to stand guard, you think.

He looks up at you. "Need anything, kid?"

"No," you say. "I was just restless."

Turn to page 76.

It's slow going—the woods along the pond are very thick. There's lots of thorny brush that's tricky to get through. You're about halfway around when you stop because the brush is so dense ahead of you.

You wonder whether to cut back into the woods or wade along the edge of the pond. You stop to think for a moment and hear something moving in the woods. You duck low and listen. Someone is coming from behind you, moving in your direction! It can't be Tom—he went around the other way. A shudder runs through you. The route back is cut off.

You could hide in the thick brush ahead, but if whatever is coming *is* a werewolf, it would probably hear you moving or smell you out. Maybe you should jump into the pond and swim to the far side.

If you hide in the brush, turn to page 25.

If you jump in the pond and swim for it, turn to page 7.

"Wh—what have you done?" Aunt Charlotte stammers.

"How—" you start to say, as the old woman comes over and takes your chin, cradling it in her gnarled, wrinkled hand. Her hand is damp and very cold. A chill goes through your whole body. You start to shiver. She lets go, but you can't stop shivering. Tom is shivering too.

Aunt Charlotte is staring at the bristly hairs on the floor. She can't seem to move.

"You look cold, dear," Mrs. Hadley says to you. "Won't you have some tea before you leave?"

"No!" you say loudly.

The woman shakes Aunt Charlotte's shoulder. "You are not frightened, are you, my dear? And to think that *you* were worried about *me*!" She bursts into a wild, cackling laugh.

"Uh, yes, we were," Aunt Charlotte says. "We thought . . ." Her voice trails off.

"We thought that it—" You point at the floor but can't finish your sentence.

Turn to page 73.

Mrs. Hadley pauses for a minute. "But you are just children—I wouldn't want to describe what he looked like."

"Tell us!" Karin says. "We're old enough."

"You probably don't know what we see on TV," you add.

She gives you an odd, quick smile. "All right, I'll tell you, if you really want to know. His neck and shoulders were raked by claws, as if some animal—"

Karin gasps. "Like the body they found at the pond!" Which is just what you are thinking.

"Did they catch the murderer?" you ask.

Mrs. Hadley shakes her head. "They combed the woods for him. And they searched the shack where the man with the pointed face lived. In it were bones—rabbits, dogs, and even—"

"Human?" you put in.

"Yes. Human." She smiles, as if she likes the idea. "This was no ordinary murderer," she declares. "This was a *werewolf.*"

Turn to page 72.

Quickly you help Karin pull one end of the bed away from the wall. Then you run around behind it. The two of you start pushing.

From the hallway comes a noise—not a howl, but a deep, throaty growl. Then footsteps. They stop right outside the door. With a final shove, you and Karin jam the bed in between the door and the corner of the closet. A second later there's a great thump on the door, then another, and another, and another. Then a furious roar!

THUMP! The latch breaks. The door springs open a few inches and jams against the bed frame. You see the dark nose, furry snout, and jaws of a werewolf! Then it backs up.

THUMP! THUMP! THUMP! You and Karin cringe in the corner, watching the door bang against the bed frame. The werewolf is getting really angry!

It stops for a moment. You hear the werewolf panting and growling in the hallway. Then he smashes the door so hard it splits the wood of the bed frame. The crack in the door opens wider. Another tremendous smash! The wood splits even more!

Turn to page 46.

You can't see clearly through the grimy panes, but you can make out someone heading toward the shack. His hair, neck, and shoulders are bristly, and his head is flattened. His long, pointed mouth is slightly open. He has the teeth and snout of a wolf!

"I'm out of here!" Tom yells. He runs out the door. You have a split second to decide what to do. Tom is already ahead of you. If you make a break for it, the werewolf could probably outrun you, and you'd be the first one caught. Maybe the werewolf is already after Tom. You could hide under the bed, then escape next time he goes out.

If you run after Tom, turn to page 44.

If you hide under the bed, turn to page 49.

"I'll go with Tom," you say.

"Hope you make it back," Karin says.

Tom cringes and makes big eyes as if he's frightened. "Don't *you* worry about *us*!" he says to her. The two of you head out the door.

Tom leads you along the road and then down a path through the woods. You pass a narrow, rutted dirt road going off to the right.

"I wonder where that goes?" Tom says. "I've never been down it."

"Maybe we should check it out," you suggest.

"Well, we're almost to the pond," Tom says. "That's where the body was found."

The two of you keep walking, and in a few moments you can see the pond through the trees. It looks about a hundred and fifty feet across. Crows are flitting in the branches on the other side.

The path comes out at a grassy area along the pond's edge, but the area is roped off. A sign hung on the rope says CRIME SCENE—KEEP AWAY.

Turn to page 52.

"I wish it *weren't* a werewolf bite," you say, pretending to be worried. "I wonder what it might do to me."

Tom stares at you for a moment, then looks again at your leg. "It is a weird-looking bite," he says. "I've never seen anything like it."

"That's because you've never been bitten by a werewolf," you say. "Not yet, anyway."

He backs up more, almost knocking over a lamp, and jumps like a frightened rabbit. Then he stands there, looking at you as if he doesn't know whether to believe you or not.

You have a feeling that from now on, Tom is going to be a little bit scared of you. He looks so worried standing there. You can't help laughing.

"What are you laughing at?" he says angrily. "I know you weren't bitten by a werewolf."

"Sure," you say. "If that's what you want to think."

Turn to page 10.

36

You've overslept a little, and when you enter the kitchen, you find that Karin is the only one there. Aunt Charlotte's car is gone—she must be out on an errand, maybe with Tom, since you don't see him around.

"Hi," Karin says.

"Hi." You hardly look at her—your eyes are on the countertop, where Aunt Charlotte has put out cereal, bananas, muffins, and juice. You glance over to see what Karin is eating. It's something very strange. You step closer. It can't be! *She's eating a mouse!*

You watch in horror as she cuts a hind leg off and takes a bite of it, as if it were a shrimp on a toothpick, or a little piece of chicken. You stand there, unable to take your eyes off it.

Strangely, your feeling of horror is fading away. Another feeling is taking hold of you: *The mouse looks delicious!*

The End

"Let's leave it on," you say.

Aunt Charlotte, stroking Karin's hair, says, "Honey, why don't you read a book in your room if you don't want to watch."

"Fine. I'll leave!" Karin jumps up and storms out of the room, not even bothering to take her popcorn.

The rest of you go back to watching the movie. The father is trying to beat the werewolf by swinging a chair at him. The lights flicker off completely. Now there's just faint moonlight in the family's room, but you can see the werewolf. He makes terrible growling noises. Suddenly he turns and jumps the father!

Turn to page 62.

"All right, I'll try it," you say.

"Good, good." Again he makes the soft, purring sound. He leans closer. You take a tiny sip. It's greasy and hot and slightly bitter. It makes you feel slightly dizzy.

"Good, isn't it?" the werewolf says. "Drink the rest!"

"No, thanks," you whisper. "I'm not feeling well."

"LEAVE!" the werewolf suddenly shouts. He throws the door open and reaches toward you as if he's going to grab you. But you're already out the door and running for your life!

You don't stop until you've reached Aunt Charlotte's. You're glad to be free, but very worried about that soup. You feel okay now, but it made you feel kind of strange when you tasted it. What did it have in it besides rabbit? What might it have done to you?

There's no way of telling. Not now, it seems. But that night, just before dawn, you wake up and walk toward the window. You stand there for a long time, staring at the moon, until, for some reason you can't understand, you let out a long, wailing howl.

The End

40

Headlights are shining up the driveway. Aunt Charlotte is back, and Tom is with her. Karin reaches the car. She pulls open the back door and dives in. You're right behind her.

Aunt Charlotte laughs. "Hey, we're not going anyplace!"

"We *have* to," Karin says, shaking. "Th—"

"You've got a bloody nose!" her mother interrupts, staring at you. She hands you some tissues. "What's going on?"

"Look!" Tom yells as a flash of lightning lights up the sky.

"Oh my lord!" Aunt Charlotte cries. You all watch in horror as the werewolf lopes through the shadows at the side of the house. Then it is dark again. A moment later, you hear a long, wailing howl.

Turn to page 6.

Karin clutches your arm as a thunderclap sounds overhead. "That's Tom!" she cries. "With the werewolf!"

"Are you sure?"

"I know my own brother!"

"But is that a werewolf?"

"It's him! I know it's him!" She lets out something between a gasp and a cry. Another flash of lightning illuminates the two figures.

"Tom!" Karin calls. *"Tom!"* Thunder drowns out her voice.

"Tom!"

There is no answer.

Karin stares at you in horror. She seems frozen with fear. You don't blame her—you want to run after Tom, but you're afraid yourself!

If you run down the road after Tom, turn to page 56.

If you decide it's wiser to run back to the house, turn to page 53.

You decide to stay at the house. Now that the policeman is here, you're actually hoping that the werewolf will come back. It would be neat if you could get a close look at him—and see him get caught.

"Now don't go wandering outside," Aunt Charlotte tells you before she leaves. "And if you hear any strange noises, be sure to let the officer know. We should be back in ten or fifteen minutes. Are you sure you want to stay?"

"Yeah, I'll be okay."

A minute later Aunt Charlotte and your cousins pull out of the driveway. You feel a twinge of regret, wondering whether you might be missing something. At the same time, you're a little nervous. What if the werewolf *does* come back? There's a policeman in the house, but he can't be everywhere at once.

You try to read a book, but you're too restless. You start wandering around the house. Standing by a window, you peer into the darkness and listen for sounds. All you can hear is the soft hum of crickets and an occasional car going by on the road.

Turn to page 28.

"Tom, stop that!" Karin says. She grabs a pillow and tries to swat her brother in the face. He throws up his arms to fend it off.

"Stop it, both of you!" says Aunt Charlotte.

Again you hear the howl. Aunt Charlotte gets up and looks out the window. "It does sound as if it's coming from outside," she says.

"Maybe the werewolf outside is hearing the one in the movie," you say.

"That's not funny," Karin says. "Someone was *murdered* near here. *Remember?*"

Suddenly in the movie, the werewolf, huge and hulking, has burst into the room. His paws are outstretched, showing long, curved claws. His jaws open, revealing sharp, spiked teeth. The family cringes in the corner.

"The phone is dead!" the father cries.

"No! No!" the mother screams.

"Can't we turn this off?" Karin pleads.

Tom yells at her, "Go to another room if you don't like it!" Then, to you, he says, "You want to watch it, don't you?"

If you say "yes," turn to page 38.

If you say "no," turn to page 70.

You take off and run as fast as you can along the rough, uneven trail. Behind you, you hear the sound of racing footsteps, then something between a growl and a roar.

You try to run faster, not wasting time to look back. You're gaining on Tom. Soon you're only steps behind him. "Faster!" you yell.

He half-turns, but then suddenly he's falling, his foot snagging on a vine! He hits the ground. You can't stop—you trip and tumble over his body.

You and Tom are both scrambling to your feet when you feel the iron grip of clawed hands clutching you. In your ear is the hot, panting breath and low, throaty growl of a werewolf! His long, toothy jaws are only inches from your neck!

You struggle to escape, but he tightens his grip even more. The werewolf shakes both of you until your strength is totally sapped, and you go limp with terror, defeat, and despair.

Turn to page 80.

"What are you thinking?" you ask.

"That maybe the werewolf did something to Tom!"

"So he won't talk to us?"

"That, or even worse." Karin shakes her head, as if trying to get her thoughts to fall into place. "Do you think we should tell my mom?" she asks. "I mean she should know, but what can she do? It'll just upset her."

If you say, "We'd better tell her,"
turn to page 84.

If you say, "I don't think we should tell her,"
turn to page 57.

"He's going to get in!" you yell to Karin. "We've *got* to get down the tree!"

She quickly climbs up onto the windowsill, but then she freezes. There's a two-foot-wide gap between the window and the tree.

It's still pouring. Lightning flashes. Thunder rumbles across the sky. "You can make it," you cry. "Get your arms and legs around the tree trunk—you can shinny down."

With a little shriek, she jumps. She grabs the tree just right and starts shinnying to the ground. You quickly climb up on the windowsill.

Behind you, there's a terrible crunch. The bed frame gives way. The door flies open. You look over your shoulder. A grizzly, hulking figure is coming at you, its jaws open, its long tongue curling over its sharp, curved teeth.

You fling yourself into the air and hit the tree hard, smashing your nose. You manage to get your arms and legs around the tree trunk. From there, it's only a second or two of shinnying down—then a three-foot drop to the ground. You almost hit Karin, who is just getting to her feet.

Turn to page 40.

The werewolf relaxes his grip, but not enough to let you move. To your horror, he starts sniffing Tom's neck and then yours! He is mumbling and growling in a low voice.

You open your mouth to scream, but he slaps his paw over it.

"Neither of you is ripe," he says. "I am going to let you go. But on one condition!"

"Anything!" Tom says quickly.

"QUIET!" he roars. "The condition is that you will forget everything you saw and heard this afternoon."

"Sure!" Tom says. "We will!"

"Yes, we will!" you cry. You're thinking how impossible it will be to forget what's happened. But that's not something you're going to say to the werewolf!

"Good." He relaxes his grip a bit more. "Because if you ever do remember what happened, then . . . *we shall meet again.* Do you understand?"

"Yes," you and Tom blurt out.

"THEN GO!"

Turn to page 69.

You're certain the werewolf will catch you if you run, so you fling yourself under the bed. You lie there listening, wondering if Tom is being chased. You hear nothing but the cawing of a crow.

The minutes tick by. You wait, sweating, wishing you were someplace else. The suspense is awful. You start wiggling out from under the bed, then freeze as you hear footsteps.

The door swings open. The werewolf has returned. He's pacing around. There are no sounds of Tom—he must have gotten away!

You don't move a muscle, but your brain is spinning in circles. The werewolf is moving about. You don't dare peek and see what he is doing—you're too close to the edge of the bed as it is. You'd try to wiggle farther back, but you're afraid of making a noise.

Then you smell smoke. It must be something cooking. It gives off a sort of greasy, meaty smell. Maybe it's a rabbit, stewing in the pot.

Turn to page 64.

"She probably went out," Tom says.

"Out? I don't think she goes out at night," his mother replies. She calls again. This time when she hangs up, she's clearly angry.

"I told the police they should send over someone to guard Mrs. Hadley. They said they had no one available—that they can't provide a guard for everyone in the town."

"Well, that makes sense," you say.

"Yes," your aunt says. "But Mrs. Hadley is old and lives alone. Something must have happened, or she would have answered the phone. I'm going over there to make sure she's all right."

"Mom, you shouldn't go out," Tom says.

"I'm going," she says. "You kids can either come with me or you can stay here with the policeman."

Turn to page 74.

He leads you back to his patrol car, where he applies antiseptic and a bandage. He tells you to go to the doctor when you get home.

You head back to Aunt Charlotte's place, limping a little. No one's there when you arrive, so you change into dry clothes, get a soda from the fridge, and lie down on the couch. Your leg feels better once you take your weight off it.

A few minutes later Tom comes in. "Hi. Where did you go?" he asks. "I was afraid the werewolf had gotten you!" He takes a look at your bandage. "Where did you get *that*?"

"I was bit."

"Not by the werewolf?" he says, his eyes widening.

"I'm not saying."

"Let me see." He edges closer.

You peel back the bandage, just far enough for him to see the marks of a bite and the bluish-black bruises around them.

"Ugh!" Tom backs away, his face showing his disgust. "That wasn't really the werewolf, was it?"

Turn to page 35.

52

"This is it all right," says Tom. "Do you think we'd get in trouble if they caught us going past the rope?"

"Definitely," you say.

"Let's do it anyway," he says excitedly. "Or should we go back and check out that dirt road instead?"

If you decide to ignore the KEEP AWAY sign, turn to page 68.

If you decide to check out the dirt road, turn to page 65.

"I don't think it's safe to go down there," you say.

"Well, we'd better get help," Karin says. The two of you race back to the house, slowing only to catch your breaths. When you get there, you can't find Tom or your aunt. You check all the rooms to make sure.

You and Karin stand by the kitchen window, watching as the rain begins to pour down. Except for occasional flashes of lightning, it's almost completely dark.

"Maybe we should call the police," you say.

The kitchen door opens.

Turn to page 60.

With a swift motion, you hurl the hot soup at the werewolf.

He screams, rubbing the thick, steamy broth from his eyes. You are about to run, but you can't help staring at him. His furry snout is taking on the shape of a human face. His teeth are shrinking. His clawed paws are beginning to look like hands. Then you notice he's crying!

You don't know what to make of this. But you don't spend time thinking—you're out the door and running like you've never run before!

You never look back. By the time you reach Aunt Charlotte's house, you're completely out of breath. You're also completely happy. You know that somehow you conquered the werewolf. And you're sure he'll never bother you again.

The End

56

"I'm going to find out what's going on," you say, and start running down the dirt road. Karin is right behind you.

You soon reach the place where you thought you saw Tom, but there's no sign of him or the werewolf. It's almost dark now. The moon casts only a few patches of light on the dusky road ahead. Now you see Tom running toward you. He yells something, but his voice is drowned out by a tremendous clap of thunder.

Turn to page 66.

You decide not to tell your aunt what you saw. After a day or so, you're glad you kept quiet. There's no more news of the werewolf, and Tom seems perfectly normal. You have lots of fun going into town to the movies, playing softball, and visiting a local amusement park.

It's only the night before you're set to leave that Tom seems a little strange, and Karin too. They've been spending a lot of time together lately. Tom looks scruffier than he used to. And there's almost a glint in his eye. Karin has been making throaty sounds and sort of loping along as she walks. It makes you kind of uncomfortable—and glad you're going home.

That night you have trouble sleeping. There's a mosquito in your room. It keeps buzzing around your ears. When you finally do fall asleep, you have terrible dreams. In one of your dreams, you feel something touching you. You feel hot breath in your ear. Then you wake up. Or you think you wake up, except that you're looking into the face of a wolf! You turn and feel claws raking your neck!

Turn to page 61.

It makes you feel better to have him there with you.

"I'm glad the storm has passed," you say, putting your hands behind your head. The policeman doesn't say anything.

"Did they teach you how to fight werewolves at the police academy?" you ask with a small laugh. No answer. You hope that your aunt and cousins get back soon.

A few minutes go by. "It's sure quiet out here," you say. Still no answer. "Can you hear me?" you ask, a little surprised by the policeman's rudeness. You get up and walk over to his chair. His badge gleams in the moonlight.

"I said, can you hear me?" you repeat, bending down to look into the policeman's hairy face. *Hairy face?!*

The policeman has become a werewolf! And you're at his mercy!

"I've heard every word you said," he tells you with an evil grin as you back away. "After all, I've got big ears now."

The End

60

"Hello!" a voice calls. Tom has returned, soaking wet. He looks as if he doesn't have a care in the world.

Karin runs to him. "Tom, are you all right?"

"Sure—why wouldn't I be?" he says, shrugging.

"We saw you in the woods," Karin says.

"With the werewolf," you say. "What was going on?"

"I wasn't with any werewolf," he says. "I was just looking for clues."

Karin, hands on her hips, glares at him. "Tom, are you sure you weren't with someone?"

"I wouldn't lie to you," he says coldly. "So leave me alone." He turns and goes upstairs, leaving you and Karin looking at each other.

"I don't know whether to believe him or not," you say.

"Neither do I," says Karin. "I could have sworn it was Tom on that road."

"And I could have sworn that was the werewolf," you add.

Karin's face darkens.

Turn to page 45.

But then you *do* wake up. You jump out of bed, scattering blankets and pillows, and stand there shaking, glad to be out of the nightmare!

You turn on the light to make absolutely sure there's no one in the room. Then you go to the bathroom and look in the mirror. There's some blood on your neck. You wipe it off. There are scratch marks and a little welt.

You must have been attacked by a werewolf! You almost let out a scream, but then you calm down. You probably were bitten by the mosquito. The bite itched, and you scratched yourself. That must be what happened.

Just the same, you leave the light on for a long while before you turn it off and finally go back to sleep.

The nightmare is only a dim memory when you wake up in the morning. You'll be taking the bus home around noon. Just thinking about it lifts your spirits. When you come down to breakfast, you feel strangely happy and energetic, as if you had just gotten over a really bad cold.

Turn to page 36.

This is one scary movie, you think. Suddenly there's a shuffling behind you. Karin must have decided to come back down. She must still be mad, though. Instead of sitting with all of you on the sofa, she takes a bowl of popcorn and sits on the big cushioned chair in the corner.

The movie continues, with everyone running around the room as they try to escape the werewolf.

Ping! Something hits you in the head. It's popcorn. Karin must be bored. But you're caught up in the movie, so you ignore her. Tom and Aunt Charlotte ignore her too.

"Heh, heh, heh," laughs Karin loudly. She snorts a few times and noisily eats some popcorn.

"Shhhh!" whispers Tom. "We can't concentrate."

Then the screen goes almost dark. But the growling and terrible noises continue—right in the room where you're sitting!

The next second, a whole bowl of popcorn comes flying through the air, landing on you, Tom, and Aunt Charlotte.

Turn to page 71.

"This movie is getting too scary!" Karin says. "Turn it off."

"No," Tom says loudly. "It's just getting good." He's hardly finished speaking when you hear a long, wailing howl.

Aunt Charlotte sits bolt upright, turning her head and cupping her ear. "Was that coming from the movie or from our woods?"

"From our woods," Tom says. *"Heh, heh, heh,"* he laughs, trying to sound scary.

Turn to page 43.

64

You hear low, throaty noises. They are much louder and deeper than a cat's purr, but they remind you of that. Maybe the werewolf is happy because he's going to eat.

You hear him moving again, stepping closer to the bed.

He's stopped. What is he doing? Please don't see me, you think.

You hear an *Ahhhhrrraugghhh!*—a growl that turns into a roar. Then you feel the iron grip of claws on your arm, pulling you out from under the bed. You look up to see the face of a *werewolf!*

With a single swift motion he lifts you up, puts you in a chair, and pushes it in front of a table. The skin of a freshly killed rabbit is stretched out on the table. There is a pot on the woodstove with steam rising from it—he's been making soup.

He ladles some out into a crude wooden bowl. Then he sits on a bench and looks at you.

"I like you," he finally says.

Turn to page 86.

"Let's go down that dirt road and see what we can find," you say.

"Okay, let's," says Tom.

The road winds through the woods, twisting as it curves up a hill. It's so rutted and washed out a Jeep couldn't even drive on it.

You come to a place where a tree has fallen across the road. From there on, the road is nothing more than a trail leading into the wilderness. You follow the trail until a few hundred yards farther on it ends abruptly in a huge pile of brush.

"I wonder who piled this up here?" you say.

Tom shrugs. "Beats me. I've never been back here before. It looks like a barrier, as if someone didn't want people to go any farther."

"Well, that's not going to stop us!" you say. "Come on!" You cut into the woods around the brush pile. Tom goes the other way, and the two of you meet on the far side. The trail continues on, but it's overgrown and hard to follow.

Turn to page 78.

Then you hear him screaming. "Run! The werewolf had me, but I got away!" He is almost beside you now. There's a flash of lightning, and in that brief instant you see blood on his collar.

Then all three of you are running, with you in the lead. You don't even stop when you reach the main road. Finally, you slow down under a streetlight.

"Is the werewolf still behind us?" you gasp between breaths.

"No," a deep, husky voice answers. "He's right beside you!"

You look over at Tom and shriek! His face has started to turn into a snout and is already covered with fur! His hands have become paws, and his fingers are sprouting sharp-pointed claws!

Turn to page 83.

"Let's stay and look here," you say.

You duck under the rope and start walking around, searching the ground for clues. Tom checks out the grassy area between the woods and the pond. You continue on to the water's edge.

Dark clouds are racing across the sky. The wind has picked up, sending ripples along the surface of the pond. You kneel and run your fingers through the water. It's cold. Glancing across the pond, you notice what looks like a path going into the woods.

Tom calls to you, "I can't find anything. They must have combed it over pretty well."

"Did you know there's a path leading to the pond from the other side?" you call back. "The werewolf might have escaped that way."

Tom squints at where you're pointing. "Yeah, I see it. I never noticed that before," he says. "We'd better check it out."

"Okay," you say. "I'll circle around the left side of the pond, and you go the other way. That way, we'll cover the whole area."

Tom nods, and you each start around.

Turn to page 29.

He releases his grip. You and Tom are on your feet and running as fast as you can until you are over the rise and out of sight of the werewolf and his shack. Finally you stop to catch your breath.

You look at Tom, and he looks at you.

"I'm remembering what happened. Are you?" Tom asks.

"How could I forget it?" you reply.

"I know," says Tom. "But that means we're not doing what he told us to."

"Who cares?" you say. "He can't read our minds."

You take a deep breath, getting ready to take off again. Suddenly you hear branches crashing. And long, wailing howls—that sound closer and closer!

You and Tom look at each other again. The werewolf *can't* read your minds. Or can he?

The End

"No, let's shut it off," you say.

"That's enough of *that*!" Aunt Charlotte grabs the remote and stops the movie. She gets up and sets the VCR on rewind.

Just then, the telephone rings, startling all of you.

"Hello?" says Aunt Charlotte. You and your cousins watch as she twists the phone cord, her mouth opening in shock. "Are you sure? Another body?" she says to the person on the phone. "With huge teeth marks?"

The End

"I don't want this, I want more MEAT!" a voice shouts.

Aunt Charlotte quickly turns on the light and then lets out a scream. It's the *werewolf* who has been sitting in the chair! You and Tom huddle behind Aunt Charlotte. Karin is nowhere in sight! You wonder if something awful has happened to her. The creature, an evil gleam in his eyes, comes toward you.

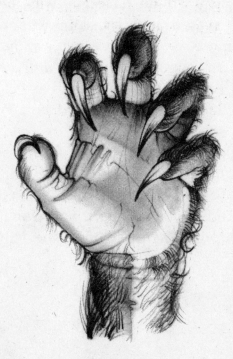

The End

"Oh!" you say. "And now he's come back!"

"For another meal," Karin adds.

Maybe more than one, you think.

"Gosh, you must have been scared," Karin says.

A thin smile forms on Mrs. Hadley's lips, but instead of making her look friendly, it makes her look frightening. "Yes, I was scared out of my wits," she says, raising her voice. "That's why I don't have any wits, *heh, heh, heh*. But even though I lost my wits, I gained something else. *There are many things I can do, my little sweets. Things you'd never dream of!*"

Karin looks alarmed. "We'd better get on home," she says nervously.

You glance out the window. Dark clouds are blotting out the last light of day.

"Yes, you'd better go home," Mrs. Hadley says. "And, if you're smart, you won't go out alone around here again, especially after dark."

Turn to page 81.

"I guess there was nothing to worry about," Aunt Charlotte says.

Mrs. Hadley's eyes are flashing, reflecting the light like the eyes of her cat. She reaches for the teapot and pours more tea. A bitter smell enters your nostrils, giving you a weird, sickly feeling, like nothing you've known.

"No, there was nothing to worry about," the old woman says in a slow, deliberate tone. "The night of the werewolf has passed, but don't think you are safe, now that—"

"Now that what?" you blurt out. But before you get an answer, Aunt Charlotte leaps to her feet, steps over to the door, and opens it. She breathes deeply from the fresh air blowing in. Turning, she says, "Come on, children. Good night, Mrs. Hadley."

"That what, Mrs. Hadley?" you ask again.

"That you've learned my secret!" the woman cries. Her mouth forms a thin, cruel smile. Her eyes hold you tightly. Her gnarled hands reach out toward you. But Aunt Charlotte is pulling at your arm. She motions to Karin and Tom. The three of you are all quickly out the door.

Turn to page 82.

"I'll come," Tom says. "I've got to protect you."

"I'll come to protect you too," Karin says.

Aunt Charlotte grins. She touches your shoulder. "Do you want to come, or would you rather stay here with the policeman?"

If you say you'll go, turn to page 27.

If you decide to stay in the house, turn to page 42.

A moment later there is a flash of lightning, quickly followed by a tremendous clap of thunder. A hard rain begins to fall.

Another flash. The lights flicker on and off, and then on again. A moment later you're startled by a violent pounding on the front door.

You and Karin run upstairs to her bedroom and look out the window. Even though it's pretty dark, you still have a good view of the front door. Whoever was knocking has disappeared.

AWAAARRREEEEEEEEEeeeeeeee! Again the howl comes—this time from inside the house!

Karin clutches your arm. "We must have left the door unlocked!"

Turn to page 15.

"Well, relax. No werewolf is going to get you with me around. Why don't you go watch TV or something?"

"Okay," you say and turn to leave.

But you don't feel like watching TV—you can do that anytime. Aunt Charlotte said not to go outside, but there's no reason you can't go on the screened porch. You step out onto it, leaving the light off so your eyes can get used to the dark. That way, if the werewolf comes prowling around, you might be able to see him.

There's a hammock, a wicker couch, and two rocking chairs on the porch. You lie down in the hammock, but it makes too much of a creaking sound, so you get up and sit on the couch. A full moon comes out from behind a cloud, casting an eerie light across the lawn.

You strain your eyes, trying to see into the shadows, wondering if anything's there. A few minutes later you hear a slight creaking from one of the rocking chairs. The policeman has come out to join you.

Turn to page 58.

Before you get there, the door opens and Aunt Charlotte walks in. You and Karin scream. Aunt Charlotte is growing long, bristly hair! Her mouth and face are turning into the snout of a wolf! She smiles, but it is not a human smile. Her teeth have grown sharper and longer. Her tongue rolls out of her mouth.

"Hello, my sweets," she says in a deep, husky voice. "Tom and I had a very interesting time together. And so will we. So will we."

The End

You and Tom continue on over a rise, down into a hollow, and up another rise. Then you stop short. Through the woods you can see a crudely built wooden shack. It has a door and a couple of small windows on either side and a stovepipe coming out of the roof.

You can feel your heart beating. This could be the home of the werewolf! You and Tom inch closer, eyes and ears alert, like deer in a forest full of predators.

The shack looks abandoned. Moss is growing on the roof. The tiny windows are covered with dust. Tangled vines climb up the sides.

"I don't think anyone's using it," Tom says in a low voice.

"We'll find out," you say, though part of you feels like turning back.

You reach the door. Its wooden planks are warped and weathered. The hinges are almost rusted off. You tap on it, ready to run if someone opens it, but there's no sound from inside. You lift the latch and push. The door opens, the hinges squeaking as if they haven't been oiled in years.

Turn to page 16.

"And I don't want Tom hanging around where such a terrible crime was committed. I'm going down there to find him. I'll be back soon. Meanwhile, you two stay put."

She heads out the door. A moment later you hear her car pulling out of the drive.

The house seems strangely silent. You stand at the kitchen window, looking out. Storm clouds fill the sky, but for a moment the moon appears, hanging low over the treetops before disappearing behind another cloud. You are about to turn away when you hear a howl—not the howl of a dog, but a great, long wailing sound.

AWAAARRREEEEEEEEeeeeeeeeee!

Suddenly Karin is next to you, her hand on your shoulder.

"What was *that*?" she says nervously.

"I don't know," you say. "It sounds like a wolf!"

AWAAARRREEEEEEEEEeeeeeeeeeee! Again you hear the howl—this time closer.

Turn to page 75.

The creature seemed more human than animal when you first saw him. Now he seems to be much more like a wolf. You are almost surprised to hear him speak, his voice low and throaty.

"What were you doing in my house?"

"N-N-Nothing," you say. "We were just curious."

"We're really sorry about this—honest," Tom says. His voice is shaking.

Turn to page 48.

There's a tone to her voice and a look in her eyes that send a chill through you. You don't want to seem chicken, but you're thinking it might be a good idea to call Aunt Charlotte and ask her to come pick you and Karin up. Maybe you should get Karin to call her.

If you tell Karin she'd better call her mom and ask her to pick you up, turn to page 26.

If you decide just to walk home, turn to page 11.

"Thank you for stopping by," Mrs. Hadley calls after you. "Next time, I'll come and visit *you!*" Her wild, cackling laugh rings in your ears as you hurry back to the car.

You all scramble in. Aunt Charlotte starts the engine.

"I can't believe what we just saw!" Tom says.

"And what we heard!" you add.

Aunt Charlotte puts the car in gear and pulls away. "I wouldn't have believed it if I hadn't seen it myself," she says.

"I *still* can't believe it," you say. "The werewolf's body on the floor . . . the way it just disappeared!"

"I don't know if I feel better or worse," Karin says.

"I think you should feel better," her mother tells her. "We don't have to worry about a werewolf anymore."

"That's true," you say. "Now we can start worrying about a witch!"

The End

"Ahhh!" screams Karin, stumbling back-
ward.

Tom smiles, and in the light of the street
lamp you see his teeth, gleaming, still growing, as they close in on your neck.

The End

84

It takes you a while to get around to it, but the next day, when Tom goes to the store on an errand, you and Karin tell your aunt about how you saw Tom with the werewolf.

She removes her eyeglasses and stares at you. "Is this true?"

"Yes," you both say firmly.

Turning to Karin, Aunt Charlotte says, "I know you wouldn't make up something like this, but I find it hard to believe. I'll have to speak to Tom myself."

Later in the day, Aunt Charlotte and Tom go for a drive. They are gone a long while—you and Karin begin to get worried about them. You feel better when you hear Aunt Charlotte's car pulling into the driveway, and you and Karin go to the kitchen door to meet them.

Turn to page 77.

You are trying to wake up, but you're very groggy. You hurt all over, and you barely have any sense of who you are or what has happened.

You're in a bed. The ceiling of the room is white, and the walls are pale green. Your leg is in a cast and is propped up in the air. Slowly, you remember.

Someone is looking in at the door—a nurse.

"How are you feeling?" she asks.

"Terrible," you say. "How is my cousin Karin? She was with me when—"

"I know. Your cousin is just down the hall, dear. She'll only have to stay overnight. She wasn't banged up nearly as bad as you were. Just a nasty bite on her forehead—took about eight stitches to sew it up."

"A *bite*?" you say slowly.

"Yes," the nurse says. "I don't know the details. A big dog, I suppose."

The End

You nod but say nothing. You don't want him to like or dislike you, you just want to get away from him! "Can I go now?" you say.

"In a minute." He shoves the bowl toward you. "First, try my soup."

You look into the dark broth. Little strips of rabbit meat and bone are floating in it. "No thanks," you say. You try to push the bowl back toward him.

He blocks it with his bristly, clawed hand. "Try my soup," he says, raising his voice. "Then you can go."

You shake your head—you don't want to eat or drink anything that's been near this creature!

Turn to page 12.

TILL YOU Laugh Scream!

With each and every one of these scary, creepy, delightfully, frightfully funny books, you'll be dying to go to the *Graveyard School!*

Order any or all of the books in this scary new series by **Tom B. Stone**! Just check off the titles you want, then fill out and mail the order form below.

☐	0-553-48223-8	**DON'T EAT THE MYSTERY MEAT!**	$3.50/$4.50 Can.
☐	0-553-48224-6	**THE SKELETON ON THE SKATEBOARD**	$3.50/$4.50 Can.
☐	0-553-48225-4	**THE HEADLESS BICYCLE RIDER**	$3.50/$4.50 Can.
☐	0-553-48226-2	**LITTLE PET WEREWOLF**	$3.50/$4.50 Can.
☐	0-553-48227-0	**REVENGE OF THE DINOSAURS**	$3.50/$4.50 Can.

BDD
Bantam Doubleday Dell
Books For Young Readers

BDD BOOKS FOR YOUNG READERS
2451 South Wolf Road
Des Plaines, IL 60018

Please send me the items I have checked above. I am enclosing $_____
(please add $2.50 to cover postage and handling).
Send check or money order, no cash or C.O.D.s please.

NAME _____

ADDRESS _____

CITY _____ STATE _____ ZIP _____

Please allow four to six weeks for delivery.
Prices and availability subject to change without notice.   BFYR 113 2/95